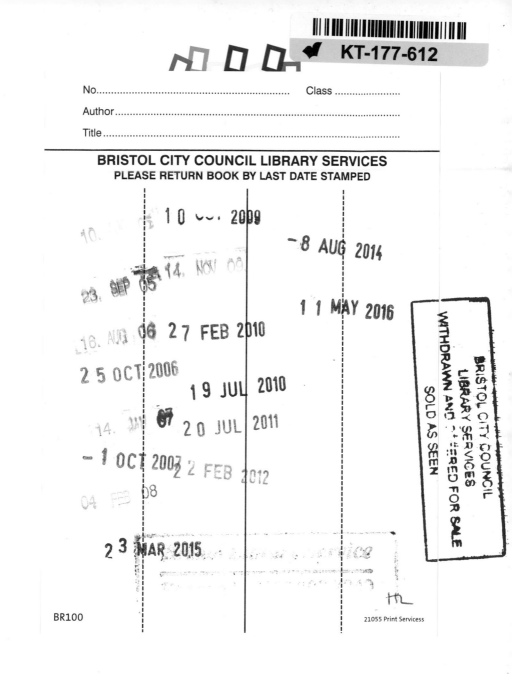

First published in 2002 by
Franklin Watts
96 Leonard Street
London
EC2A 4XD

Franklin Watts Australia
56 O'Riordan Street
Alexandria
NSW 2015

A CIP catalogue record for this book is available
from the British Library.

ISBN 0 7496 4700 0 (hbk)
ISBN 0 7496 4707 8 (pbk)

Series Editor: Jackie Hamley
Series Advisor: Dr Barrie Wade
Cover Design: Jason Anscomb
Design: Peter Scoulding

Printed in Hong Kong

"Sausages!"

by Anne Adeney and Roger Fereday

FRANKLIN WATTS
LONDON•SYDNEY

Once there was a poor man called Albert who needed some new shoes.

5

Albert asked the village shoemaker to make him some fine, new shoes.

But when they were ready, he couldn't pay for them.

"It's clear that you don't have enough money to pay for these shoes," said the shoemaker.

"But I know how you can pay and it won't cost you a penny," he added, with a smile.

"How?" asked Albert.

"From now on you must only say one word, 'Sausages!'" the shoemaker told him.

"You mustn't say anything else until we meet again!"

"Sausages!" agreed Albert and he hurried home.

"You're late," grumbled Albert's wife. "What have you been doing?"

"Sausages!" replied Albert.

"What did you say?" she asked, crossly.

"Sausages! Sausages!" Albert
shouted, trying not to laugh.

Albert's wife was worried. She
rushed next door to ask her
neighbour for help.

"Come quickly!" she yelled.
"There's something wrong
with Albert!"

The neighbour hurried next door.
"What's wrong, Albert?" she asked.
"Can I get you anything?"
"Sausages!" came the reply.

"He's lost his mind!" wailed Albert's wife.

"I'll fetch the mayor," promised the neighbour. "He might help!"

The mayor came to visit Albert.

"What's the problem?" he asked.

"Sausages!" replied Albert.

"What?" shouted the mayor.

"Sausages!" Albert said again,

feeling very silly.

Soon the whole village knew that there was something wrong with Albert and he could only speak nonsense. Albert was embarrassed.

The next day, the mayor visited the shoemaker.

"Have you heard the news?" asked the mayor. "Albert has gone mad!" "Rubbish!" replied the shoemaker.

24

"He has!" said the mayor, crossly. "He only says 'Sausages!' when you talk to him! He makes no sense!"

So the shoemaker played his little
trick. "I bet you fifty gold coins
that Albert is not mad," he said,
knowing the mayor was rich.

"It's a deal," agreed the mayor,
and they went to find Albert.

"Hello, Albert!" said the shoemaker.
"Sausages! – oh, I am pleased to see
you!" answered Albert. "Now I don't
need to say 'Sausages!' any more.

The whole village thinks I'm mad
because of this sausage talk. These
shoes have certainly cost me a lot!"

"Not as much as they've cost the mayor!" the shoemaker laughed, as the mayor handed him fifty gold coins.

So the shoemaker was paid for his shoes after all. Now Albert pays his bills on time. And the mayor has never made a bet again!

Hopscotch has been specially designed to fit the requirements of the National Literacy Strategy. It offers real books by top authors and illustrators for children developing their reading skills.

There are 12 Hopscotch stories to choose from:

Marvin, the Blue Pig
Written by Karen Wallace, illustrated by Lisa Williams

0 7496 4473 7 (hbk)
0 7496 4619 5 (pbk)

Plip and Plop
Written by Penny Dolan, illustrated by Lisa Smith

0 7496 4474 5 (hbk)
0 7496 4620 9 (pbk)

The Queen's Dragon
Written by Anne Cassidy, illustrated by Gwyneth Williamson

0 7496 4472 9 (hbk)
0 7496 4618 7 (pbk)

Flora McQuack
Written by Penny Dolan, illustrated by Kay Widdowson

0 7496 4475 3 (hbk)
0 7496 4621 7 (pbk)

Willie the Whale
Written by Joy Oades, illustrated by Barbara Vagnozzi

0 7496 4477 X (hbk)
0 7496 4623 3 (pbk)

Naughty Nancy
Written by Anne Cassidy, illustrated by Desideria Guicciardini

0 7496 4476 1 (hbk)
0 7496 4622 5 (pbk)

Run!
Written by Sue Ferraby, illustrated by Fabiano Fiorin

0 7496 4698 5 (hbk)
0 7496 4705 1 (pbk)

The Playground Snake
Written by Brian Moses, illustrated by David Mostyn

0 7496 4699 3 (hbk)
0 7496 4706 X (pbk)

"Sausages!"
Written by Anne Adeney, illustrated by Roger Fereday

0 7496 4700 0 (hbk)
0 7496 4707 8 (pbk)

The Truth about Hansel and Gretel
Written by Karina Law, illustrated by Elke Counsell

0 7496 4701 9 (hbk)
0 7496 4708 6 (pbk)

Pippin's Big Jump
Written by Hilary Robinson, illustrated by Sarah Warburton

0 7496 4703 5 (hbk)
0 7496 4710 8 (pbk)

Whose Birthday Is It?
Written by Sherryl Clark, illustrated by Jan Smith

0 7496 4702 7 (hbk)
0 7496 4709 4 (pbk)